MR. MEN
LITTLE MISS
The Christmas Elf

Roger Hargreaves

Original co...
Roger Har...

Written and illustrated by
Adam Hargreaves

Everyone was busy at the North Pole.

The reindeer were doing their daily exercises to get fit for their long journey.

The Christmas elves were making toys and wrapping presents.

And Father Christmas was busy checking his list.

A list of who had been naughty and who had been good throughout the year.

A list of who was going to receive a Christmas present and who was not.

And to make sure he didn't forget, Father Christmas wrote everything down in a book.

A very big book!

Father Christmas is a very generous, kind and jolly person and because of this, he is very forgiving.

You have to be very, very, very naughty to get a red cross beside your name in his big book.

How naughty do you have to be?

Well, you have to be so naughty that in fact there is only one name in the whole of Father Christmas' enormous book with a red cross beside it.

And can you guess that name?

It was Little Miss Naughty.

Of course!

The scale of Little Miss Naughty's naughtiness was such that Father Christmas could hardly believe it.

Could anyone possibly be that naughty?

So, he decided to send one of his elves to double-check.

And what that elf saw was one long catalogue of naughtiness from Boxing Day all through the year to Christmas Eve.

And, as the elf discovered, the closer it got to Christmas, the more naughty Little Miss Naughty got.

She stole all the tinsel in town!

She filled the mince pies with sour lemons.

Father Christmas' elf could not believe her eyes.

She even got caught up in all Little Miss Naughty's naughtiness!

And the result of all this naughtiness was no Christmas present for Little Miss Naughty.

Ever.

Not once had Father Christmas visited her house!

However, Little Miss Naughty had a plan to change this.

A sensible plan would have been to behave, but Little Miss Naughty had no such intention.

You will not be surprised to hear that her plan involved a lot more naughtiness.

Just before Christmas, she flew to the North Pole.

And her elf followed.

A very worried elf.

What was Little Miss Naughty going to do?

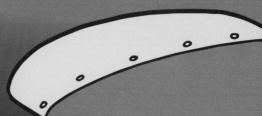

The first thing she did when she arrived was to sabotage Father Christmas' sleigh.

Poor Father Christmas!

But this was not part of Little Miss Naughty's plan.

She just could not help herself!

Then she jumbled up all the presents.

This was also not part of her plan.

Luckily the elves managed to fix Father Christmas' sleigh and unjumble all the presents in time for Christmas Eve.

However, that night Little Miss Naughty crept into the room where Father Christmas kept his book.

Now, this was Little Miss Naughty's plan.

She was going to rub out the red cross beside her name and replace it with a green tick.

She chuckled to herself as she heaved open the cover of the enormous book.

It would be so easy!

But it wasn't. For it was a very, very big book. And it was a very long list of names.

Little Miss Naughty ran her finger down the first page.

No Little Miss Naughty.

She turned to the next page.

Still no Little Miss Naughty.

She turned page after page after page.

On and on she read.

It dawned on Little Miss Naughty that this was going to take a very long time.

A remarkably long time.

And a thought occurred to Little Miss Naughty's elf as she watched Little Miss Naughty turning the pages.

She told Father Christmas and he realised that she might be right.

So, they left Little Miss Naughty to her search.

It did take a very long time.

Longer than Little Miss Naughty could ever have imagined.

It took …

… a whole year! A whole year of turning pages. A whole year of reading names.

Until finally, on Christmas Eve, she found her name.

"At last!" she cried.

"At last, indeed," said Father Christmas, who reached over and put a green tick beside her name.

"You've done it!" cried Little Miss Naughty's elf. "A whole year of not being naughty."

Which was what she and Father Christmas had hoped for all along. And so, that year Little Miss Naughty received her very first Christmas present.

But very probably …

… her last!